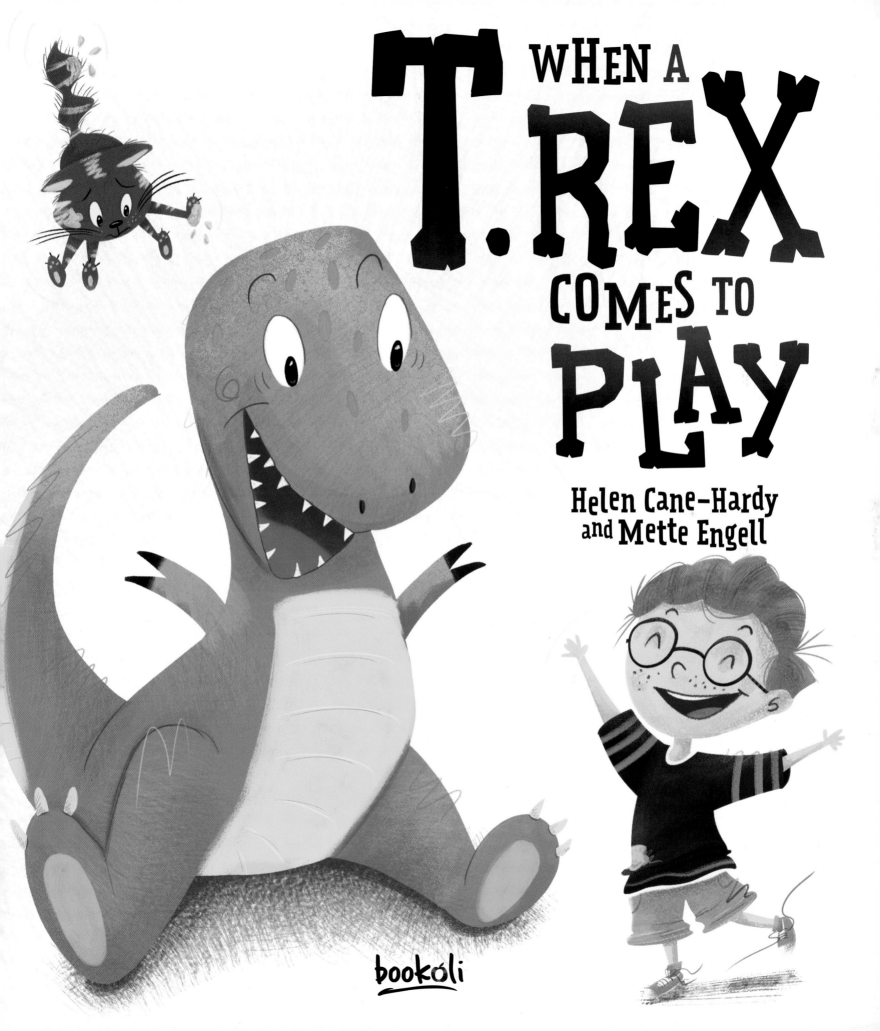

WHEN A T.REX COMES TO PLAY

Helen Cane-Hardy
and Mette Engell

bookoli

It was the summer break for Pip
and he wanted something **FUN** to do.

He loved being with his baby sis,
but was sick of playing
PEEK-A-BOO!

One warm day, feeling bored at the park, he saw a **TAIL** behind a bush.

Then came an **ARM**...

a **HEAD**...

and a **LEG**.

It was a ...

... T. rex saying,

"SHUSSSSSSSSH!"

He stood up tall on his scaly claws, and said, "I am **soooo boooooored** today.

If I promise not to **SNAP** my jaws, could I come round to play?"

"At last, **SOME FUN!**"
thought Pip, feeling smug.
"But Mama will never say yes."

So with a scarf, he made
a disguise,

and used his blanket as
a dress.

"What shall we play?" asked Pip at the house. T. rex saw Pip's cat and **SMILED,**

"CATCH-A-SNACK is my very best game..."

But that game turned way too WILD!

T. rex **STOMPED** into the kitchen and **STAMPED** ketchup on the floor.

He **ate the cakes** Pip's mama had baked,
then searched the cupboards for **more**.

"I think that's enough
to eat," said Pip,
and took T. rex to find some **toys.**

But while Pip was looking through boxes,
T. rex started to make a **NOISE...**

His tummy RUMBLED, GARGLED and FIZZED,
as he gulped a strawberry tart.
His cheeks turned a mighty shade of pink
and he did an enormous

FART!

T. rex **crashed** into the bathroom and pooped an **ENORMOUS** dino **TREAT.**

Then he sat down in the bathtub
and started to clean his **DIRTY FEET.**

"This is not going to plan," thought Pip.
"It's tough having a **DINO FRIEND.**"

But how do you tell a big **T. REX** that it's time for the fun to **END?**

Now Pip was **clever**, Pip was **smart**, an idea lit up his brain...

He gave **T. REX**
some skates to wear

and watched him whizz off down the **LANE!**

The house turned quiet. The house turned still.
Pip looked at the mess on the **FLOOR**.
"Next time I'll stick with peek-a-boo,
and stay away from friends who

ROAR!"